Where the River Begins

WHERE THE RIVER BEGINS

by Thomas Locker

A Puffin Pied Piper

PUFFIN PIED PIPER BOOKS
Published by the Penguin Group
Penguin Books USA Inc., 375 Hudson Street, New York, New York 10014, U.S.A.
Penguin Books Ltd, 27 Wrights Lane, London W8 5TZ, England
Penguin Books Australia Ltd, Ringwood, Victoria, Australia
Penguin Books Canada Ltd, 10 Alcorn Avenue, Toronto, Ontario, Canada M4V 3B2
Penguin Books (N.Z.) Ltd, 182-190 Wairau Road, Auckland 10, New Zealand
Penguin Books Ltd, Registered Offices: Harmondsworth, Middlesex, England
Originally published in hardcover by Dial Books
A Division of Penguin Books USA Inc.

Library of Congress Catalog Card Number: 84-1709
Printed in Hong Kong by South China Printing Company (1988) Limited
First Puffin Pied Piper Printing 1993
ISBN 0-14-054595-6
1 3 5 7 9 10 8 6 4 2

A Pied Piper Book is a registered trademark of Dial Books,
a division of Penguin Books USA Inc.,
® TM 1,163,686 and ® TM 1,054,312.

WHERE THE RIVER BEGINS
is also available in hardcover from
Dial Books.

To the memory of my teacher Joshua C. Taylor

Once there were two boys named Josh and Aaron who lived with their family in a big yellow house. Nearby was a river that flowed gently into the sea. On summer evenings the boys liked to sit on their porch watching the river and making up stories about it. Where, they wondered, did the river begin.

Their grandfather loved the river and had lived near it all his life. Perhaps he would know. One day Josh and Aaron asked their grandfather to take them on a camping trip to find the beginning of the river. When he agreed, they made plans and began to pack.

They started out early the next morning. For a time they walked along a familiar road past fields of golden wheat and sheep grazing in the sun. Nearby flowed the river – gentle, wide, and deep.

At last they reached the foothills of the mountains. The road had ended and now the river would be their only guide. It raced over rocks and boulders and had become so narrow that the boys and their grandfather could jump across.

In the late afternoon, while the sun was still hot, the river led them into a dark forest. They found a campsite and set up their tent. Then the boys went wading in the cold river water.

The first long day away from home was over. That night,
around the flickering campfire, their grandfather told Josh and
Aaron stories. Drifting off to sleep, they listened to
the forest noises and were soothed by the sound of the river.

Dawn seemed to come quickly and the sun glowed through a thick mist. The boys were eager to be off, but their grandfather was stiff from sleeping on the ground and was slower getting started.

The path they chose led them high above the river. On a grassy knoll they stopped to gaze around. The morning mist had risen and formed white clouds in the sky. In the distance the river meandered lazily. It was so narrow that it seemed almost to disappear. They all felt a great excitement, for they knew they were nearing the end of their journey.

Without a word the boys began to run. They followed the river for an hour or more until it trickled into a still pond, high in an upland meadow. In this small, peaceful place the river began. Finally their search was over.

As they started back, the sky suddenly darkened. Thunder crashed around them and lightning lit the sky. They pitched their tent and crawled inside just before the storm broke. Rain pounded on the roof of their small tent all night long, but they were warm and dry inside.

In the morning long before dawn they were awakened by a roaring, rushing sound. The river had swelled with the storm and was flooding its banks. They tried to take a shortcut across a field but were soon ankle deep in water. Grandfather explained that the river drew its waters from the rains high up in the mountains.

They came down out of the foothills in the soft light of late afternoon. The boys recognized the cliffs along the river and knew they were close to home. Their weariness lifted and they began to move more quickly down the road.

At last they reached their house on the hill. The boys raced
ahead to tell their mother and father about the place where the
river began. But their grandfather paused for a moment and
in the fading light he watched the river, which continued on as
it always had, flowing gently into the sea.